First published in Great Britain in 2009 by Dean,
an imprint of Egmont UK Limited,
239 Kensington High Street, London W8 6SA
Based upon the television series Bob the Builder
© 2009 HIT Entertainment Limited and Keith Chapman
All rights reserved. The Bob the Builder name and character,
related characters and the Bob figure and riveted logo are
trademarks of HIT Entertainment Limited.
Reg. U.S. Pat. & ™. Off. And in the UK and other countries.

ISBN 978 0 6035 6417 8
Printed in Italy
1 3 5 7 9 10 8 6 4 2

Bob's Boots

One morning, Bob received
a parcel from the postman.
"I wonder what's inside?"
said Bob.

"Oh great! My new boots."

Bob walked out into the yard,
proudly wearing his brand
new work boots.

Squeak, squeak!
Bob heard a sound, and stopped to listen. But when Bob stopped, so did the squeaks.

"Oh, er . . . **is it mice?**"
worried Lofty.
"No, don't worry, Lofty," laughed
Wendy. "It's Bob's boots.
They're **squeaking** because
they're new."

Meanwhile, at the farm, Spud and Travis were arguing about the quickest way to get to Bob's yard.

"Turn **left** at the crossroads," said Spud.

"No, turn **right**,"
said Travis.
"I'm sure **left** is the **right** way,"
said Spud.
"How can **left** be **right**?"
asked Travis, very confused.

They asked Farmer Pickles to decide. "The quickest way is usually as the **crow flies**," he said.

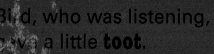

Bird, who was listening,
gave a little **toot**.

"Sorry, Bird," laughed Farmer
Pickles. "It means going in a
straight line, like a bird flies.
Now come on, Travis, we've got
work to do."

Spud turned to Bird. "I can walk faster than any old bird can fly!" he boasted. "I'll **race you** to Bob's yard."

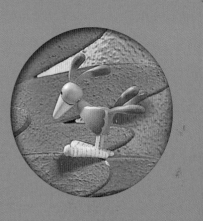

"**Toot!**" said Bird, and off he flew.

Spud followed Bird, looking up to the sky as he walked, but he wasn't looking where he was going and accidentally tumbled over a wall!

Lofty and Bob were fitting a new gate at the farm. Bob was looking forward to his packed lunch, a cheese and chutney sandwich

and a cream bun.
"My favourite!" Bob said.
As he opened his lunch
box, a big gust of wind
blew his paper napkin
away. Bob and Lofty
chased after it.
Squeak, squeak, squeak!
went Bob's boots.

As Spud was running along
after Bird, he noticed a lunch box
on the ground. He stopped and
took a look inside.

"**Yeuk**, **chutney!**" said Spud.

Spud didn't like the taste of Bob's
cheese and chutney sandwich.
But the big cream bun looked
yummy! "I'll **save that**, and
eat it later," he said.

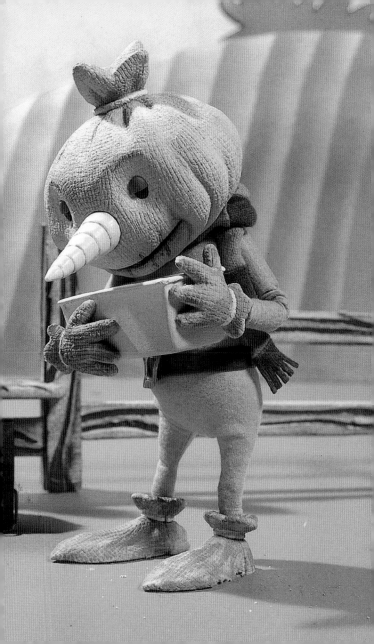

"**Toot!**" said Bird,
flying past Spud.

"**Wait for me!**"
said Spud.

Bob was still busy trying to
catch his napkin. **Squeak,
squeak, squeak!** went his boots.

Bob didn't notice that some
mice were following his
squeaking boots.

"**Eek, eek, eek!**"
the mice squeaked.

"Ohh, **phew**, got it Lofty,"
said Bob as he finally caught
his napkin.

"**Oh, that's good!**" said Lofty.

"I'm ready for my lunch,
after all that running about,"
laughed Bob. "Hang on,
who's been eating my lunch?"

Bob was looking for his cream
bun when Lofty saw the mice
near Bob.

"**Arrrgh! M-m-mice!**" he wailed.

Lofty ran off and Bob chased after him. "Come back, Lofty. It isn't mice, it's only my boots!" he shouted.

Squeak, squeak, squeak! went his boots.

"**Eek, eek, eek!**" went the mice.

Lofty raced back to the yard
and stopped in front of
Roley and Dizzy.
"Ohhh, no! Mice!"
squealed Lofty.

Roley looked shocked.
"What's going on, Lofty?"

"Oooh, behind me," cried Lofty.

As Bob ran into the yard, Lofty pointed to the mice behind him.

"**Look, Bob!**" he said. "**M-mice!**"

"**Eek, eek, eek!**" went the mice.

"You were right, Lofty! They must like my **squeaky boots**," said Bob.

When Spud ran into the yard,
he saw the mice, too.
"**Arrrgh!**" he said, dropping the
cream bun on the floor.
"**Mice! I'm off!**"

The mice squeaked out of the
yard, following Spud.

"So, that's where my lunch
disappeared to!" exclaimed Bob.

"Bob, have you noticed?" chuckled Wendy. "Your boots have stopped **squeaking!**"

"So they have. I must have worn them in with all that **running** around," said Bob.

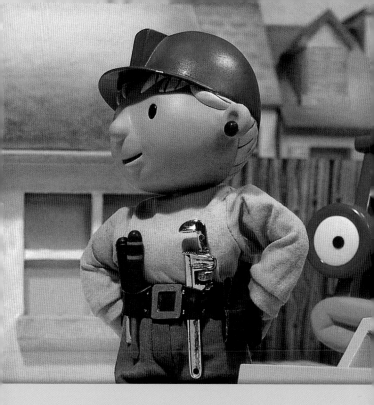

"You've had a busy day then?"
asked Wendy.

"Not really . . . you could say
it's been as **quiet as a mouse**,"
laughed Bob.